伊善
YEH-HSIEN

retold by Dawn Casey

illustrated by Richard Holland

Simplified Chinese translation by Sylvia Denham

古代书卷中传说从前在南中国有一个女孩，名叫伊善。
她从小便聪明仁慈，长大后因为妈妈和爸爸相继死去，
她便由继母接管照顾，她亦因此认识到什么是极度哀伤。

继母自己也有一个女儿，她不喜欢伊善，只供应极
少量的食物给伊善，让她穿破旧褴褛的衣服，
强迫她到最危险的树林去捡拾柴枝，到最深的水池取水。
伊善只有一个朋友…

Long ago in Southern China, so the old scrolls say, there
lived a girl named Yeh-hsien. Even as a child she was
clever and kind. As she grew up she knew great sorrow,
for her mother died, and then her father too. Yeh-hsien
was left in the care of her stepmother.

But the stepmother had a daughter of her own, and had
no love for Yeh-hsien. She gave her hardly a scrap to eat
and dressed her in nothing but tatters and rags. She forced
Yeh-hsien to collect firewood from the most dangerous
forests and draw water from the deepest pools.
Yeh-hsien had only one friend...

一条有红色鳍金色眼的小鱼儿。伊善最初认识他时，他的确是很细小的，但她用食物和爱心喂养小鱼，他很快便逐渐长成一条巨大的鱼。
每当伊善来到池塘时，鱼儿总是把他的头抬起来枕在她旁边的池畔。
没有人知道伊善的秘密，直至有一天她的继母问自己的女儿：
「究竟伊善把她的米饭拿到那里去呢？」
她的女儿建议说：「你为什么不跟踪她看看？」

于是，继母躲在一丛芦苇后面，等候着，观察着，当她看到伊善离去时，她把手猛推进水池来回拨动。「鱼啊！鱼啊！」她低声哼吟，但是鱼儿安然留在水底。「可恶的家伙，」继母咒骂著说，「我会将你…」

...a tiny fish with red fins and golden eyes. At least, he was tiny when Yeh-hsien first found him. But she nourished her fish with food and with love, and soon he grew to an enormous size. Whenever she visited his pond the fish always raised his head out of the water and rested it on the bank beside her. No one knew her secret. Until, one day, the stepmother asked her daughter, "Where does Yeh-hsien go with her grains of rice?"
"Why don't you follow her?" suggested the daughter, "and find out."

So, behind a clump of reeds, the stepmother waited and watched. When she saw Yeh-hsien leave, she thrust her hand into the pool and thrashed it about. "Fish! Oh fish!" she crooned. But the fish stayed safely underwater. "Wretched creature," the stepmother cursed. "I'll get you..."

「你工作得真辛苦！」继母后来对伊善说。「你应该
得到一条新裙子。」她跟着要伊善换去破旧的衣服。
「现在就去水泉处取水，无须急著赶回来。」

当伊善走了之后，继母立即穿上褴褛的衣裙，
赶到池塘去，收藏在她的衣袖里面的是一把刀。

"Haven't you worked hard!" the stepmother said to Yeh-hsien
later that day. "You deserve a new dress." And she made
Yeh-hsien change out of her tattered old clothing. "Now, go
and get water from the spring. No need to hurry back."

As soon as Yeh-hsien was gone, the stepmother
pulled on the ragged dress, and hurried to the
pond. Hidden up her sleeve she carried a knife.

鱼儿看到伊善的裙子一阵子后便把头伸出水面，跟着继母插下匕首，
鱼儿庞大的身躯拍动出池塘，躺在池畔，死去了。

「真美味，」继母晚上一面烹煮鲜鱼肉，一面洋洋得意地说，
「他的味道比普通的鱼好吃得多。」继母和她的女儿把伊善的朋友的
每一块肉都吃光了。

The fish saw Yeh-hsien's dress and in a moment he raised his head out of the water. In the next the stepmother plunged in her dagger. The huge body flapped out of the pond and flopped onto the bank. Dead.

"Delicious," gloated the stepmother, as she cooked and served the flesh that night. "It tastes twice as good as an ordinary fish." And between them, the stepmother and her daughter ate up every last bit of Yeh-hsien's friend.

第二天，当伊善叫喊她的鱼儿时，一点应声也没有，当她再叫时，
她的声音变得奇怪尖锐，她的腹部感到收紧，嘴巴干涩。
伊善用手膝拨开浮萍，但什么也看不到，只有卵石在阳光下闪烁着，
于是她知道她唯一的朋友已离去了。

可怜的伊善哭泣哀号著跨倒在地上，将头埋在手里，
因此看不到一位老人从天上飘降下来。

The next day, when Yeh-hsien called for her fish there was no answer. When she called again her voice came out strange and high. Her stomach felt tight. Her mouth was dry. On hands and knees Yeh-hsien parted the duckweed, but saw nothing but pebbles glinting in the sun. And she knew that her only friend was gone.

Weeping and wailing, poor Yeh-hsien crumpled to the ground and buried her head in her hands. So she did not notice the old man floating down from the sky.

一阵微风吹向伊善的眼眉，她那红肿的眼睛往上望，那老人俯视着她，
他的头发松散，衣服粗糙，但是他的眼睛充满着慈爱。

「不要哭，」他温和地说，「你的继母把你的鱼儿杀死后，
将骨头埋藏在粪堆里，快去，取回鱼骨，它们有神奇的魔力，
无论你祈望什么，它们都会赐给你的。」

A breath of wind touched her brow, and with reddened eyes Yeh-hsien
looked up. The old man looked down. His hair was loose and his clothes
were coarse but his eyes were full of compassion.

"Don't cry," he said gently. "Your stepmother
killed your fish and hid the bones in the dung
heap. Go, fetch the fish bones. They contain
powerful magic. Whatever you wish for, they
will grant it."

伊善遵照老人的指导，把鱼骨藏在她的房间内，她经常把它们拿出来，紧握着它们，鱼骨在她的手里感到平滑、清凉和沉重。她大多数是怀念她的朋友，但有时也会许一个愿望的。

现在伊善有她所需要的所有食物和衣服，还有珍贵的玉石和皎洁的珍珠。

Yeh-hsien followed the wise man's advice and hid the fish bones in her room. She would often take them out and hold them. They felt smooth and cool and heavy in her hands. Mostly, she remembered her friend. But sometimes, she made a wish.

Now Yeh-hsien had all the food and clothes she needed, as well as precious jade and moon-pale pearls.

很快又飘逸着梅花的芬香，意味着春天的来临，这正是春节联欢时间，人们都团聚一起向祖先表示敬意，年轻男女亦希望能找到丈夫和妻子。
「我多么渴望能参加啊，」伊善叹道。

Soon the scent of plum blossom announced the arrival of spring. It was time for the Spring Festival, where people gathered to honour their ancestors and young women and men hoped to find husbands and wives.
"Oh, how I would love to go," Yeh-hsien sighed.

「你?！」她的异母姐妹说，「你不可以去！」
「*你*必须留在这里守果树，」继母命令她说。
就是那样决定了。或者未必，如果伊善不是那么有决心的话。

"You?!" said the stepsister. "You can't go!"
"*You* must stay and guard the fruit trees," ordered the stepmother.
So that was that. Or it would have been if Yeh-hsien had not been so determined.

当继母和姐妹走了之后，伊善立刻在鱼骨前跪下许愿，愿望即时获得赏赐实现。

伊善穿上织锦袍服，她的斗蓬是用翠鸟的羽毛造成的，每一根羽毛都耀目生辉，当伊善走来走去时，每一根羽毛都闪烁着各种不同的蓝色 – 靛蓝色、青金蓝、翠蓝色、以及她的鱼儿居住的池塘所散发的阳光闪耀湖水蓝。穿在她脚上的是一双金鞋子。她优美得像随风摆动的杨柳，她就这样摇曳生姿地飘然去了。

Once her stepmother and stepsister were out of sight, Yeh-hsien knelt before her fish bones and made her wish. It was granted in an instant.

Yeh-hsien was clothed in a robe of silk, and her cloak was crafted from kingfisher feathers. Each feather was dazzling bright. And as Yeh-hsien moved this way and that, each shimmered through every shade of blue imaginable – indigo, lapis, turquoise, and the sun-sparkled blue of the pond where her fish had lived. On her feet were shoes of gold. Looking as graceful as the willow that sways with the wind, Yeh-hsien slipped away.

当她靠近春节联欢会时，伊善感到地面循着跳舞的节拍震动，
她可以闻到烧烤嫩肉和醇酒的香味，她可以听到音乐、歌唱和笑声，
她所看到的都是人们正在愉快欢乐中，伊善也展露高兴的笑容。

As she approached the festival, Yeh-hsien felt the ground tremble with the rhythm of dancing. She could smell tender meats sizzling and warm spiced wine. She could hear music, singing, laughter. And everywhere she looked people were having a wonderful time. Yeh-hsien beamed with joy.

很多人都转过头来看美丽的陌生人。
「那女子*是*谁？」继母盯着伊善奇怪地问。
「她看来有点像伊善，」异母姐妹皱着眉困惑地说。

Many heads turned towards the beautiful stranger.
"Who *is* that girl?" wondered the stepmother, peering at Yeh-hsien.
"She looks a little like Yeh-hsien," said the stepsister, with a puzzled frown.

伊善感觉到各人都凝视着她，她转过头来发觉自己正在面对著继母，她的心情冷却，微笑顿失。
伊善快速地离去，在急忙中，她的一只金鞋子脱落了，但她不敢停下来捡拾，于是赤着一只脚一直跑回家去。

Yeh-hsien felt the force of their stares and turned around, and found herself face to face with her stepmother. Her heart froze and her smile fell.
Yeh-hsien fled in such a hurry that one of her shoes slipped from her foot. But she dared not stop to pick it up, and she ran all the way home with one foot bare.

当继母回到家时，她看到伊善正在双臂拥抱着园中的一株树干熟睡。她凝视着继女一会儿后便哼声笑说：「哼！我怎会怀疑*你*是联欢会的那个女子呢？荒谬！」跟着她便不再细想了。

那只金鞋子又怎样呢？它掉在长草之间，被雨水冲洗，被露水滴湿。

When the stepmother returned home, she found Yeh-hsien asleep, with her arms around one of the trees in the garden. For some time she stared at her stepdaughter, then she gave a snort of laughter. "Huh! How could I ever have imagined *you* were the woman at the festival? Ridiculous!" So she thought no more about it.

And what had happened to the golden shoe? It lay hidden in the long grass, washed by rain and beaded by dew.

清晨时份，一名年青男子在薄雾中漫步，金色的闪光令他眩目。
「这是什么？」他拾起鞋子喘着气说：「…很特别的东西啊。」
那名男子把鞋子带到邻近的度安岛，将它献给那里的国王。

「这鞋子真是精巧别致，」国王惊异地说，并将鞋子放在手中把弄。
「如果我能够找到适合穿这样的鞋的女子，我亦找到一个妻子了。」
国王命令皇宫内各个女人试穿鞋子，但鞋子的尺码比最细小的脚还小一寸。
「我会在整个国土内找寻，」他誓说道。可是依然没法找到一只脚合适。
「我一定要找到适合穿这只鞋的女子，」国王郑重声明，「但是怎样找呢？」
最后他有一个主意了。

In the morning, a young man strolled through the mist. The glitter of gold caught his eye. "What's this?" he gasped, picking up the shoe, "…something special." The man took the shoe to the neighbouring island, To'han, and presented it to the king.

"This slipper is exquisite," marvelled the king, turning it over in his hands. "If I can find the woman who fits such a shoe, I will have found a wife." The king ordered all the women in his household to try on the shoe, but it was an inch too small for even the smallest foot. "I'll search the whole kingdom," he vowed. But not one foot fitted. "I must find the woman who fits this shoe," the king declared. "But how?"
At last an idea came to him.

国王和他的侍从将鞋子放在路旁，然后躲起来，看谁来领取它。
一个衣衫褴褛的女子偷偷地把鞋子取走，国王的侍从都以为她是
个小偷，但是国王却盯着她的脚。
「跟踪她，」他细声说。

「开门！」国王的侍从一面敲打伊善的家门，一面叫喊。
国王搜查屋内最深入的房间，找到伊善，她的手正拿着金鞋子。
「请穿上它，」他说。

The king and his servants placed the shoe by the wayside. Then they hid and
watched to see if anyone would come to claim it.
When a ragged girl stole away with the shoe the king's men thought her a thief.
But the king was staring at her feet.
"Follow her," he said quietly.

"Open up!" the king's men hollered as they hammered at Yeh-hsien's door.
The king searched the innermost rooms, and found Yeh-hsien.
In her hand was the golden shoe.
"Please," said the king, "put it on."

当伊善走去她的收藏处时，继母和异母姐妹都看得张大嘴巴，
伊善回来时已穿上羽毛斗蓬和她那双金鞋子。她美若天仙，
而国王亦知道他已找到他的至爱了。

跟着伊善便与国王结婚，婚礼有花灯、旗帜、锣鼓、
和最美味的食品，大婚庆典持续了七天。

The stepmother and stepsister watched with mouths agape as Yeh-hsien
went to her hiding place. She returned wearing her cloak of feathers and
both her golden shoes. She was as beautiful as a heavenly being. And the
king knew that he had found his love.

And so Yeh-hsien married the king. There were lanterns and banners,
gongs and drums, and the most delicious delicacies.
The celebrations lasted for seven days.

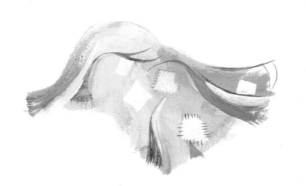

伊善和国王拥有他们希望有的一切东西。一天晚上，
他们把鱼骨埋葬在海边，让浪潮将它们冲走。

鱼儿的灵魂得释，能永远在阳光闪耀的海上游泳。

Yeh-hsien and her king had everything they could possibly wish for. One night they buried
the fish bones down by the sea-shore where they were washed away by the tide.

The spirit of the fish was free: to swim in sun-sparkled seas forever.